11/2019

School of Fish
Friendship on the High Seas

By Jane Yolen

Illustrated by Mike Moran

Ready-to-Read

Simon Spotlight
New York   London   Toronto   Sydney   New Delhi

SIMON SPOTLIGHT
An imprint of Simon & Schuster Children's Publishing Division
1230 Avenue of the Americas, New York, New York 10020
This Simon Spotlight edition September 2019
Text copyright © 2019 by Jane Yolen
Illustrations copyright © 2019 by Mike Moran
For information about special discounts for bulk purchases, please contact
Simon & Schuster Special Sales at 1-866-506-1949 or business@simonandschuster.com.
Manufactured in the United States of America 0719 LAK
10 9 8 7 6 5 4 3 2 1
Library of Congress Cataloging-in-Publication Data
Names: Yolen, Jane, author. | Moran, Michael, 1957– illustrator.
Title: Friendship on the high seas / by Jane Yolen ; illustrated by Mike Moran.
Description: Simon spotlight edition. | New York : Simon Spotlight, 2019. | Series:
School of fish | Series: Ready-to-read | Summary: Having a friend makes going to school
easier, but anxiety and fear creep back in when a little fish finds too good a hiding place
during a game.
Identifiers: LCCN 2018060006 | ISBN 9781534438910 (pbk) | ISBN 9781534438934
(hardcover) | ISBN 9781534438927 (eBook)
Subjects: | CYAC: Stories in rhyme. | Friendship—Fiction. | Fishes—Fiction. |
Schools—Fiction.
Classification: LCC PZ8.3.Y76 Fri 2019 | DDC [E]—dc23
LC record available at https://lccn.loc.gov/2018060006

I'm sleek. I'm cool.

I'm off to school.

My pencils are stacked.
My lunch box is packed
with yummy snacks
right from the sea
for my new friend
and for me.

She's waiting too,
lunch box in fin.
We play tag tail
but not to win.

We have great fun.
We're never dry.
We have a band
that's called the Fry.
We count to ten
when there's a scare.
We care.

The shark bus comes.

I'm cool as ice.

The seats are soft.

The tides are nice.

I'm silver. I'm cool.

I'm off to school.

We wait our turns
and get off the bus.
We leave
with very little fuss.

We're early yet
for our fish school.
My friend and I—
we're pretty cool.

We start a game
of hide-and-seek.
First I hide.
She doesn't peek.

I find a spot
behind a stone.
I slip into a shell,
alone.

In this big ocean, she can't see any part of fishy me.

Time swims by.
It feels like a year
that I have been
in hiding here.
What if a real shark
is very near?

Or what if she
has heard the bell
and left me hiding
in this shell?

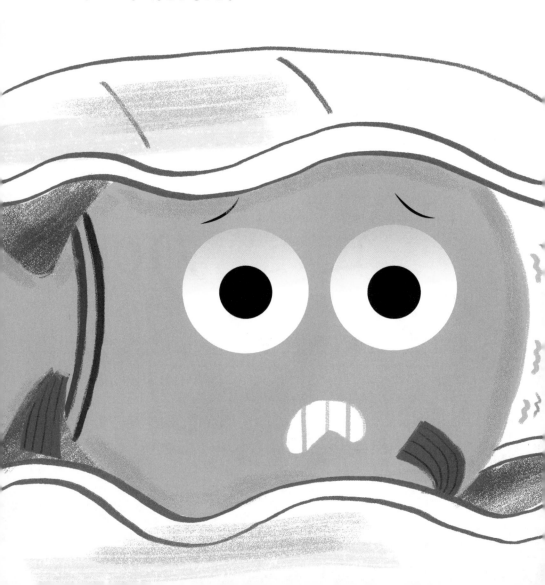

What if she thinks
that I'm too slow?
That I don't know
just how to go
with the flow?

I close my eyes
and count to ten,
think about calm seas,
and then . . .

I slowly drift
into the tide,
opening my eyes
real wide.

I see her bright pink
tail ahead.
I am no longer
filled with dread.

I know that she's
a friend of mine.
I know that everything
is fine.

Then a passing barracuda
BUMPS
into my fin.
I hear two THUMPS!

My lunch box drops
and opens wide.
Snacks disappear
into the tide.

I turn aside
and try to hide.
And, I admit,
I may have cried.

I feel a fin

upon my spine.

Another tail

now twists with mine.

My friend says,

"Hey, we *all* can share."

WE ALL?

I look to see

who else is there . . .

... *three* new friends
for me at school.

We're steady.

We're ready.

And we're *all* real cool.